How They Loved Their Gardens

Christine Trüb

How They Loved Their Gardens
Translated by Mark Miscovich

1st Edition

KBR
Greenville
2020

Publisher **Noga Sklar**
Translation **Mark Miscovich**
Text edition **KBR**
Cover design **KBR, over paintings by Frederick Frieseke (1874-1939)**

Title of the original in German *Die Liebe der beiden Frauen zu den Gärten*
Originally published by Limbus Verlag (2011).

ISBN: 978-1-944608-97-2
eISBN: 978-1-944608-98-9

Library of Congress Control Number: 2020943322

FIC027000 - Fiction/ Romance, General

KBR Digital Publishers LLC.
contact@kbrdigital.com

Published with the support of

swiss arts council
prohelvetia

Early went I in the garden
A branch caught my eye
Blossoming snow white
Oh, how my heart burned with joy.

From an old folk song

I.

A small white note with a woman's name on it. An address and a telephone number. In parentheses, the dialing code for Germany. Soon, she thinks, soon. And she puts the slip of paper, which she looks at for a while, lost in thought, several times a day, back where she has kept it from the beginning, right in the front of the book with the white cover and the blue lettering which she had started reading again a week ago, *Une vie discrète*. In February she had been planning to just browse through a bookshop in the Rue des Ecoles in Paris when she paused for a long time in front of the new releases table, instantly captivated by the first sentence. "At a bus stop, a handsome, lively, elderly gentleman hands a slim gray-blond woman a small white note with the words written on it: 'He says it's okay if you call her.'" The woman in the book has been anxiously awaiting these words. She thanks the man. They give each other a hug and three quick kisses on the cheek — right, left, right — as the bus approaches from the avenue and stops. The woman is the only person who gets on.

The people in the nearby retirement home have yet to rise from their midday nap, the schoolchildren are sitting in the classrooms of the nearby grammar school, and the guests in the restaurant across the street are paying the check. Shortly after two. Before the woman takes a seat on the nearly empty bus, she glances back. The man waves with his outstretched arm and then walks away quickly in the direction of the elongated building, built around 1880, in which his parents live in two interconnecting rooms. In one of them his father, who turned 91 today, lies in bed, and in the other his mother stands in front of the high window and watches with a pounding heart as her son returns. In the meantime, his father has closed his eyes. Has isolated himself. Made himself inaccessible.

*

The woman in the bus doesn't look at the note. She rides to the train station and from there takes a train back to Paris. She looks out the window without seeing anything — although she knows the gardens are magnificent at the end of May.

*

The characters in the novel seem somehow familiar to her as if she had met this handsome elderly gentleman and the slim gray-blond woman before, somewhere, sometime. This woman could be herself. She sees, as if it were yesterday, the bus coming up the tree-lined avenue and herself standing there holding a small white slip of paper. It was 1996. She wasn't going to Paris; she lived somewhere else, in a different country. And like the woman in the novel, she hesitated. For days. She knew she would let a hitherto stranger into her life who, from now on, would occupy an irrevocable place in it. But did she really want this? Did she want to intrude on the story of two lovers, one that had been kept secret from her for many years until her sister, visiting from her home abroad, had shouted, almost triumphantly, across the table she was sitting at with her child, an infant, that he, their father, this man that everyone thought they knew so well, he, a faithful husband, no, he had a lover, had for many years now, "don't you know that"? And she had remained calm for the sake of the child sitting on her lap who meant so much more to her at that moment than the uncovering of hidden secrets.

She only remembered the oppressive, inexplicable silence she felt in that country house where the old couple had lived for years, the fulfillment of a lifelong dream, a big house full of spacious rooms with high ceilings as if made for the happiness that strangely failed to materialize, and where sometimes the phone rang, echoing three times in a row down the long hallway before falling silent, and later, when the wife went to town to do the shopping, the husband, contrary to habit, talked endlessly on the telephone, and where happened what never should have happened. And that his wife, if the words hadn't failed her, might have told the story something like this: early in the morning, I take a leisurely stroll through my garden. Every day. In my long quilted bathrobe covered in flowers, my bare feet in a pair of soft and cozy terry-lined slippers, I walk out along the beds, green, lots of green; inside, the velvet floor-length curtains, the green fabric of the upholstered chairs, and pink — light, dark, preferably vieux rose, antique pink — inside the colors of flowers and leaves, and outside now, at the end of May, the blossoming roses, the luscious green. From inside he calls that the tea is ready. He reads the newspaper and I butter my bread; an old couple, together for forty years, fifty years since we were in the same class together at grammar school. To-day is Tuesday, no, Wednesday. He'll go into town and visit his tiny office on the top floor of an office building in one of the main streets while I take care of the house and the garden, clean up his study, and empty the heavy Bohemian ashtray. Newspapers and clippings everywhere. Tobacco crumbs. An open book. A letter for a bookmark. So, what's he reading? A book of memoirs in English. I don't recognize the handwriting. Blue pen, what bad taste. Pretty postage stamp, soft green, antique pink. Deutsche Bundespost. Next to it an ink stamp. Welcome to Bad Wörishofen in Allgäu. Allgäu? We've never been there. The envelope on top of the open book. Handy bookmark, an empty envelope. Empty? It doesn't feel like it. A letter from the Allgäu region where we've never been. Must be a young historian who wants to know something about World War II. Esteemed doctor, so on and so forth.

A different form of address. The same one I used during times of temporary separation. "Darling …" The content isn't about children or everyday matters; it talks about books, English ones, and about how marvelous the stroll had been, recently, on the bank of the river, at the end, sentences like the ones I used to write, "can hardly wait to see you again," and "always live by my side." Where? In Allgäu? Here, here, by my side. Here. There. I'm no longer sure about my favorite colors. Soft green, antique pink. The attraction of this foreign postage stamp. A black ink stamp. And wavy lines. Waves. Black.

Or did it happen some other way? Did

she accompany him to town, to his tiny office, where she intended to wait on him while he checked on something in a library, and suddenly the thought crossed her mind that the missing key to a chest of drawers she'd been looking for in vain since the move might be in the top drawer of this shabby desk, and she opened the drawer, looked for the key, and instead found a letter in an unknown hand and from a foreign country — a love letter? She begins to read it, hastily, shocked, confused, stuffs it in her handbag, closes the open drawer, leaves the room, calls later to say that she didn't want to wait until he came back to the office and that she'd gone home and is expecting him for lunch.

*

— As usual, he came home for lunch. The soup had to be on the table at twelve-thirty sharp. Normally he would start eating as soon as he sat down; he never waited until I'd served myself. But today I greeted him with the letter in my hand. I stood in the hallway when he came in and thrust the letter towards him. "What is this?" "Who is this woman?" His face changed expression and his hand swung as if he were chopping something in half, separating a head from its body. "Be silent! It's ancient history. A long time ago. What do you want to hear? Yes, I had a lover, for six years. It's got nothing to do with us." —

*

His attempt to downplay it, his refusal to explain, his silence he will never break while the rug has been pulled out from under her feet. A crack has opened into which she fears to look, behind which the facts of life no longer add up to a whole, shaking everything to the core. Her image of herself is torn with no other to replace it, and he, her husband, who knows but doesn't want to know because he fails to recognize himself, and the image of himself he has created, framed for the public, gives way to another that he has encountered in novels and his favorite books. He doesn't want to be a character in a novel; he hides his other life, "une vie discrete," at the side of a woman who lives far away. It should never have happened that a letter was found, and a secret was uncovered. No, this should never have happened.

*

— I screamed, I cried, my head seemed to be exploding. I left the table aged by years and felt the need to lie down. Only with great effort did I make it to our marital bedroom and the twin beds between which a fathomless abyss had opened. I didn't dare look down. The beds sat there next to each other, unmoved, joined by a wooden headpiece; the same beds we had bought forty years ago and in which three of our children had been conceived. I can't stand the warm shade of wood with its beautiful grain. I don't want to hear this creaking anymore when he rolls his heavy body from one side to the other. I'll move away, be alone for a while, retreat into myself. —

*

And since then she hasn't stopped looking for a deeper meaning, searching for pieces of the puzzle, without finding any, and experiencing a stabbing pain behind her forehead as if a small lead ball was ricocheting around inside her skull. And in the big rooms of the country house, this dense silence, and this shrill ringing of the telephone, three times in a row, and then silence. Inexplicable and uncanny.

*

I sat under the blooming lilac at the very back of my small garden oasis. I read in one of his letters, "… the days pass by, and I live on your letters, telephone calls, and the prospect of future rendezvouses." He has been sending me a sign of life, "my dearest love," almost every day now for the last six years. I had come home from the publishing house for a short lunch break — a sandwich under the lilac bush, a love letter — before I had to return to work. I had left the window open. I heard the phone ring, ran into the house, picked up the phone, and, out of breath, said, "Yes?" He'd never called at this time. He always likes to rest after lunch. I know because he wrote me that he always wants to be alone, close his eyes, and think about us. "This should never have happened," he said. "It was horrible." She had met him at the door with the letter in her hand. "What is the meaning of this?" She had ranted and sobbed. She had called him a liar, a cheater, and said the children would all turn their backs on him. She had locked herself in the bedroom and had refused to come out for a long time. "From now on, it's going to be difficult. We'll have to think of something." "It'll work out, don't worry," I said to him and was distressed myself. I closed the window — the garden having grown dark — put the letter with the others in the chest, hurried to the publishing house, and proofread the translation of an English text. It was an author I hadn't known, a woman from Edinburgh, I'll tell him about her — tell him? When? "From now on, it's going to be difficult," he had said. I didn't eat anything that evening; I just lay awake and waited on his call for a long time.

Will she leave him? Will they separate? Will he finally be able to come here and see where I live and work? Sit with me in my small garden, drink tea in comfort at my round, rusty table, sleep by my side at night, wake up next to me, and take me in his arms? Now that I'm finally alone, no longer having to care for my mother who passed away. Physically frail, mentally clear right up to her last breath, a devout Catholic who would have never condoned my love affair. I couldn't confide in her. To the last she had reminisced about my husband who had fallen on the Russian Front and leafed through old photo albums. "That's you in early years. Look at how dark your hair was." "What a serious, kind person, your husband, fell at the front shortly before you were to give birth. Your boy didn't survive. You were distraught at the time." "This is my favorite photo. A thin young man with glasses and short hair, and I in a light-colored summer dress — we're holding hands, standing there like children." Mother loved this picture. Now she is dead, and I'm fifty-one. Now I could furnish a room for him, a study; he would read to me what he writes before it goes to press. The apartment would be full of the aroma of his pipe tobacco. What kind of picture am I painting here? What kind of daydreams have I been spinning?

*

— "I'll shoot myself," he said. "I'll shoot myself if you leave me." Why doesn't he want me to go? Why doesn't he want to separate for a while? This "I'll shoot myself." I'm not even sure if there is a gun in the house and where he put it. There are a lot of things I can't find since we moved here and fulfilled our dream of renting a big old house with square, high-ceilinged rooms, a rose garden, and a smaller hidden garden with trellises and a meadow which blooms from March until October. Inside, long flagstone hallways and rooms with old parquet floors in dark and light geometric patterns, tile stoves, and fireplaces. We've never lived in such a beautiful place. Amidst an old stock of trees. We don't pay much on account of the owner wanting to rent the house as soon as possible after her husband hanged himself. Not here, somewhere else. Sometimes we feel that he visits us at night, startled awake at the wolf's hour by the sound of footsteps. A house full of memories. At one time a doctor lived here who used to let some of his private patients stay with him. So many stories, so much suffering. These days the grandkids run through the house and the long hallway on the second floor where the small table stands with the telephone. Our closest friends know they have to let the phone ring a long time, but sometimes it rings three or four times — I've never really kept count — and just as you reach the stairs, it stops. When it rings two or three times, it's hardly worth getting up, but you never know, so you get up, walk to the door, and as soon as you make it to the steps — silence. It rang three or four times at the most. —

*

We've agreed on a sign. How else could we stand being apart so long until our next rendezvous? Of course, I travel as often as possible to his city. I've found an inexpensive boardinghouse. The woman is nice, and she doesn't ask much for the room. If she can, she gives me the same narrow slit of a room each time, even though I don't care. I have to budget my money for the costs of travel (it takes me seven hours with the layover in Buchloe) and room and board, although I often eat something small in my room, or on a park bench when the weather allows. I know the city better than many of the locals. I hardly ever go on vacation. During the last six years, we would occasionally go somewhere beautiful for a couple of days. He wanted to show me his country. I'm always racking up overtime at the publishing house, so I can take a few days off at short notice.

There haven't been a lot of chances to spend the night together out of town: a gathering of historians or a conference at which he was speaking (his wife never accompanies him). He always says she isn't interested in contemporary history, not like me who takes a keen interest in politics and history and reads every sentence he writes. Yes, I not only read all of it, but I collect it and organize it. I'm building an archive, and I always slide the suitcase under the bed after placing something in it. I'm the only one who knows about it. People will thank me later on. Later? Why do I write this? Maybe he'll outlive me. I'm in such a dreary mood. No one here. "From now on, it's going to be difficult," he said. As if it's been easy up to now. Two incredible days, and then long separations and dry spells. Letters, yes, and telephone calls, long conversations on the phone. I let it ring three times and hang up. Our agreed upon sign when we have something to say. He calls back as soon as he can. Recently a friend visiting me said how horrible it is when the phone rings and as soon as you pick up, the person hangs up. It makes you wonder what the person was thinking. I suddenly thought, to hell with her, this friend who talks about her much older husband, how he is deteriorating mentally, and how unbearable her days have become. I was only half-listening because I had to keep thinking of him alone in the big house — his wife had gone to town — waiting on my call. Conversations, letters, a rendezvous in person? "From now on, it's going to be difficult." Oh, God.

*

— God, how am I supposed to survive this? And no one I can confide in. A stabbing headache, day and night. "Talk to me. Talk to me. What have I done wrong? Explain it to me. I can't go on living next to you like this." And he: "It's over. It's all over. There's nothing to explain. You haven't done anything wrong. You belong to me." And I scream that I'll kill myself. And he: "No, you won't. Think of the children, of the grandchildren," and I know he's right. He makes me tea in the morning, reads, smokes, works on a new book, and goes into town to his tiny office. He leads a regular life. He's friendly and doesn't let on that anything is wrong. But when I want to talk about how all this happened, where he met the woman, who she is — young, beautiful? — he looks at me as if I were speaking a language he doesn't understand, he who is so eloquent. "Be quiet, please. Don't ruin our life." I, ruin? Our long life together. His determination and his courage, which I have admired since I was young, fearless, this "I'll shoot myself," I believe him. I read a lot of novels; he, too. Fontane and then the Russians, Bunin and Goncharov. "We belong together," his sentence, over and over again.

We are somebody in this town, have a stimulating circle of friends, and an interesting life. We've never been rich — I've always made my own evening gowns as well as the curtains for these high windows here, pink silk, green velvet. It really is nice in this house. I don't want to see anymore. I have trouble getting up in the morning. It's never been easy for me as I've always needed a lot of time in the morning. I'm always worried about something because I sympathize so with people. Not him. He is a book person. He only really loves a few people. Two or three friends. The children. The grandchildren. Me. No one else. Or maybe he does. Let's leave the word love out of it. Outside, the lilacs are blooming. —

*

"Nature celebrates." Where does it say that? His birthday is today. I've almost always gone to see him. Have found some way to go. Except when his birthday fell on a Sunday; then I wouldn't visit him on the actual day, but the day before. Have always surprised him with a new release I'd read about in the London Times. Have pinned a lilac blossom on the lapel of my jacket. He inhaled its fragrance with exaggerated gallantry. A display of his love. He always managed to meet me. He used to introduce me as a colleague from Germany to chance acquaintances we met in town. A greeting, a handshake, and yes, someone said, the city is definitely worth seeing. I couldn't have asked for a better tour guide. A colleague from Germany, no one ever doubted a word he said.

And I'm no striking beauty. When I'm at home far away from him, I look in the mirror and sometimes wonder what he sees in me.

She, on the other hand. He showed me a picture once, and I was impressed. A symmetrical face, elegant, a bit aloof as if she observed life from a balustrade — I read something similar somewhere. (Is this the way people look who are still young at heart?) If I had to compare her to a flower, she would be a lily — a single white lily in a well-kept garden. No one would think of a flower when they see me.

"A real lady," I cried out in astonishment. He knew why I used the English word "lady," and since then that is how we refer to her. Today is Saturday, his birthday. "You don't have to come," he said. "We won't be able to see each other." The lady won't let him out of her sight.

*

— I watch him. I don't trust him anymore. "He who lies once…" This awful saying I used to tell my children, terrible. But I was just deluding myself. Whenever I felt unhappy, I imagined it was just in my head; I suppressed my pain and suffering and tried to fight it. Now, now I look all around, and I don't find anything, not the slightest. My unhappiness fills the rooms. If only they were smaller and less numerous, not so spacious, not so high, not so bright; if there were only a cramped, narrow hallway and a general lack of space; and if I could cover the big gold-framed mirror, the one he is standing in front of now and straightening his tie, the one he got as a birthday present from one of his daughters — he admires her exquisite taste. He pockets the pipe I got him, a Charatan this time. "It's lovely," he said gently, looked at me as always, and added that he was going into town. An unfamiliar voice answered, "I'm coming with you." —

*

I haven't heard from him all day. It doesn't help knowing he is thinking of me and that I could recite his last letter by heart, "If you knew how much I miss you." It's no substitute for the real thing. I didn't even go shopping; I just called my cleaning lady and asked her to pick me something up. I turned down a friend's invitation and simply sat there waiting for his call. I beseeched this black Bakelite phone, staring at it as if it could act on its own. His voice, just a few minutes, his deep warm voice, his gentle humor, with one of his witty sayings, sometimes in verse — he could always make me laugh. It sometimes happened that I would be simultaneously laughing and crying, as a parting always lay ahead. "I thought you once again wonderfully young and radiant, though I, like you, are reminded of the impending separation while we first embrace. I cannot cast the thought aside with a carpe diem" — he didn't want to see me cry, and he couldn't bear knowing I was sad. Look forward to our next meeting. Those words no longer reassure me. Not anymore. I don't even know when — when?

*

— We drove into town, had coffee, and then went for a walk. In the arcades, we stopped briefly to chat with some acquaintances, but with others, he simply tipped his hat, nodded, and they smiled back at me in a friendly way.

I've been the woman at his side now for forty years, and nine years before that I entered the class in which he sat in the first row. I was the new pupil — shy, blushing — and all morning he kept turning back and staring at me with his gray, unwavering eyes. I ran home at lunch, outraged. That same year I stood up and spoke in his defense as he was once again accused of — most of the teachers hated him — what was he accused of? I only remember I knew he was innocent, and that for once he wasn't the guilty party, although, yes, most of the time he was. He preferred to take the punishment than bend to authority. He has always been uncompromising, his entire life. The whole family, all six of us, had to move and start over in a new town when he felt that his work was not appreciated as it should be, when incompetents, as he said, criticized his articles. He feels superior to most people, and maybe he is. He has a tremendous wealth of knowledge, but he would be lost without me. He wouldn't be able to work. He leaves things at home to me, and that's the way I always wanted it, although I would have liked things a little easier, less strict. Living with him has never been easy. —

*

I would have loved a life like that. Stays abroad, travel, interesting acquaintances, and always at the side of a strong public figure, a man known beyond the borders of his own country. When we first met, what I felt was admiration, unreserved admiration. I'll never forget those two hours enjoying tea and scones by the fireplace, the conversation with him, his probing eyes.

On the previous day he had held a lecture on the two years leading up to the outbreak of World War II. Germans, Englishmen, Swiss, French, and some Russians who had left their country, a Czech couple, a Hungarian. A meeting place in the south of England. We both loved the country and its language. After the war I studied English language and literature, and I would have loved to have lived in London. The next day, on a stroll across the grassy dunes, we took turns listing what we knew and loved about London, and we quizzed each other, "do you know this, that…and this, too?" And we always answered with "yes, of course, certainly." Neither he nor I thought about a future; a man I would never forget, nothing more.

*

— He wants to pop into the office to look for something. "I'll go along and wait for you, flip through the newspaper — have you found it?" "No, it must be at home after all." After lunch he laid down as usual — a half hour, a full hour, sometimes just a quarter hour, depending on his work — but today I still hadn't heard anything after an hour. When I went to check on him, he said he wasn't feeling well and wanted to remain lying there for a little longer. He asked me to call him when I was making tea. It's hard for me to be alone. What happened six or more years ago? Why doesn't he finally get up? The garden is so nice. Soon, it'll be covered in shade. —

*

I haven't been outside the whole day. I have lots of time. Lots and lots of time to think about everything, but it's pointless all this thinking. It simply raises questions revolving solely around him, like how is he doing, will he ever have a moment's peace again, what kind of life will he be forced to lead from now on, and will I have to vanish from his life. He won't call anymore today. Heartless, the beauty outside, the light. My wild enchanted garden. What's the use?

*

— "Are you feeling better?" We're sitting in this rectangular garden enclosed on three sides and only visible from the neighboring meadow where sheep are grazing. It would be no exaggeration to call it Eden-like. I don't want to be expelled from it. My whole body hurts. No, that's not it exactly; rather, it seems to be chopped into pieces. Feet hard to squeeze into shoes, legs burdened by weights, and my belly as if bloated, my upper body dissected, shoulder blades stiff, and these useless breasts — I only breastfed my first child and not for very long. I had an insatiable need for beauty, intactness — where did it come from? How he admired me, and how proud he was to take me out. He never had to worry about me saying or doing the wrong thing. He had always hated the ordinary. I had gone to university, was fluent in French and English, played the piano, and could receive guests properly. I read all the books he gave me. At the front, three letters. I knew what they meant. Blue ink on off-white, the beautiful hardbound edition, a lover, six years long, like the husband of Mrs. O., of Mrs. W., charming women, but a little stuffy. I don't want to compare myself to others — am I not unique? How often had he stressed not to make a scene — was I difficult? When we were first married, maybe. Just no scene today; he hates that the most. I got furious sometimes as a young wife. Always this complacency, this superiority, and when I could have used an attentive face, comforting words, someone to listen to my concerns — the sick children, the impertinence of the maid, the lack of money — when I complained in any way, he hid behind his books and was dismissive and unapproachable.

The first year of marriage was awful. Sometimes I would run away in the evening, desperate; the river was nearby. I don't know what I'd expected of marriage. I don't remember. Undying affection, perhaps? Tenderness and warmth? What could it have been? I knew him and how disciplined he was, his enthusiasm for his work, his stubbornness, too. I would never have picked a weakling. I knew young aristocrats with impeccable manners and gentle, old-fashioned charm. One lived in a castle and managed the family's assets, nothing more. It would've been nice sometimes to be put on a pedestal. Then I compared him with my sister's husband, this tall gentleman with his long white hands and the precious ring. He couldn't stand being compared to him, he said, full of contempt. Rich boy, scaredy-cat, anti-Semite, and stingy, too. He loathed him, and my sister is my best, my closest friend.

We talk on the phone every day and usually we see each other, too. Just now he said to me, "I don't like it when you talk to your sister about us." —

*

Dream

She dreamt that the wealthy relatives and the couple with their kids were living in an enormous house on a hill. The couple lived on the ground floor, while the relatives occupied the upper two floors. A big event was coming up. A young man was going to introduce his bride. Many guests were expected. A magnificent feast had been laid out, and the servants were rushing to and fro.

The couple was sitting side by side on the sofa in the living room. The man was wearing a black suit, and the woman, a dark silk dress. They were waiting for their invitation. They were almost certain the rich sister would walk in any minute and escort them upstairs to the party. The first guests were starting to arrive. No one came for them. More and more guests were driving up the driveway. Still nothing. They heard chairs being pulled back, and it seemed that the meal was about to begin. The couple sat downstairs, getting more and more depressed by the minute. The woman and the man realized that the festive meal would take place without them. They sat there sad, two dark figures, and listened to the sounds above them. They collapsed slowly like a house of cards. The poor relatives.

(Which they really were for a long time.)

*

Sometimes, he complained bitterly. Always these relatives. Easter, Christmas, Pentecost, most birthdays, and whatever else throughout the year. Whenever they invited us with all these degenerate bores and always on the wrong side. He had to listen to things like, "Now, we can finally travel to Greece," that was after the coup. The wealth, the expensive furniture, the constant checking of stock prices, and at the same time, these philosophical, religious books all around. "Dreadful, if you only knew, but I have no choice." Once he even said that she probably loved her sister more than him.

*

Dream

She is standing by a scenic lake. Her mother and her mother's sister are bathing close to the shore. They are naked and holding each other tightly. Their white bodies shimmer under the surface of the water. Above water their long hair flows — the blond of the sister, and the brunette of the mother. They gaze up at her in a flattering, enticing manner. She turns away, shocked and full of disgust. Behind a group of tall trees, she sees a male figure whom she assumes is her father. Lonely, he paces back and forth, lost in thought. She stands there forlorn between the shore and the tall trees.

*

— How I long for someone to confide in, for my sister, but at the same time, I'm not sure if she's the right person for this kind of confidence. I don't know if faced with the constantly recurring fact of infidelity, a thousand times a day, whether a certain amount of hate wouldn't be mixed in with her heart-rending sympathy. Hate towards the man I haven't stopped loving, hate towards the man, the caveman, whom she thinks she sees in almost every man. "The wrist," she said once, "look at the wrist," and then she has some other theories about eyebrows and earlobes. There is nothing caveman-like, not the least, in the face of my husband, nothing wrong with his wrists, and his mouth, this insatiable red jellyfish — how we laughed when she mocked one of the men she had gone out with. No, his mouth is nothing like those who always seemed to fill her with disgust. His mouth is still like that of the young schoolboy who hadn't kissed a girl yet. My mouth also doesn't look like it has been joined with his for years (I've seen Rodin's sculpture and was awestruck by it). All the children, including the miscarriages, the nights in hotels, on trips, the summer holidays — our last child was conceived on a freshly mown meadow of dry grass. Why does our mouth look like it's clueless? My sister's mouth is different; a fruit, taste me, you won't regret it. Today I saw the first strawberries of the year at the market. The best time of the year. —

*

One time we ran into a flashy-dressed woman in town. She wore an open light gray fur coat and underneath a low-cut dress with a long string of pearls. She was flaxen-haired, fair-skinned, and no longer young. Some people turned to look at her. It was morning, market day, and the women were carrying baskets and tote bags. She was also carrying a basket like the rest, but that was the only thing she had in common with them. It was as if it were her first time at the market, as if she had servants at home and was mingling with the common folk for the fun of it so she could return home with a few eggs and some spring salad, winter having been over for some time now. At a flower stall not far from her front door, she found mimosas, the first mimosas from the Côte d'Azur, and this is how we ran into her, light blonde, with this bouquet of mimosas in the crook of her arm. He paid her a compliment; she kissed him on both cheeks and said, "Say hello to my sister." She looked at me with complete indifference. A name that meant nothing to me, not melodious, not a name you should know, no titles like von and zu, nothing that rang a bell in my memory. A forgettable name. I was relieved.

"You know some pretty women," I said to him after a few meters. — "That was her sister." — "Does the Lady look like her?" — "No."

*

— A year — or longer? My sister said she had run into him recently. In the company of a woman. He had mentioned a name and said it was a colleague from Germany. He was show-ing her around the city. Did she say something about "arm in arm" or "something intimate"? I don't think so, but I don't remember. If he had something to hide, I doubt he would've strolled through the old, little-used street in which my sister lived in this tall house with the enormous rooms and the terraced gardens down to the river. What a fantastic view. I didn't pursue it any further; he knows so many people. Suddenly I was sure. It was her, the other woman. This certainty was maddening. An unbearable pain. Away, just away, far away. And then these three words, this unspeakable sentence, like a thick rope encircling me, binding me, robbing me of my freedom. —

*

"I'll shoot myself." (Which of the big cozy rooms was witness to this statement? In which of the draperies did it get tangled up?) And not, "I'll kill myself." So that she could have thought about how, which method, and whether he would do it, as long as the threat contained something vague, something indefinite, uncertain. He had never struck her as a dreamer; imagination was not really one of his strong suits. She was the one who could let her thoughts wander. A waste of time, he would say. For him, deeds followed thoughts. "I'll shoot myself." His usual decisiveness. She had admired it from the beginning. Even now there was admiration mixed in with her fear. End it in a matter of minutes. That would be like him.

She believed him. She had always believed him. From the beginning. And this beginning was long ago.

The way the girl entered the classroom, he knew it had to be her and no one else. What insolence the way he — sitting in the first row of desks — kept turning his head to look at her, completely indifferent to his schoolwork and the teacher. "He stared at me," she who had sat in the last row and wished she could make herself invisible. She was very shy back then when she transferred from the Latin school for girls to grammar school. "One-track-minded, naughty brat." She blushes over her cup of hot chocolate, the same blush as eighty years ago, made up of her bashful pride in this very first meeting and her bashful courage to talk about it so frankly at her advanced age. The same blush, but not the same eyes as back then. An entire life can be read from their particular expression. The births of their four children. And most recently, eight years before the birth of her youngest grandson, the letter. The unspeakable letter. Turning points, visible in these eyes. Where else? Body language, of course, but that also has to do with the years, with the weights in the form of bags and baskets hanging on her arms, her legs getting heavy. With the slight hunch in her back and the bend in her neck.

"I'll shoot myself." A clear statement. She, on the other hand, had always had trouble thinking clearly. And now more than ever. Now that the rock she had taken him to be, steadfast in the landscape, had crumbled, a massive pile of rubble, revealing never-before-seen veins and colors. The familiar image of her life having been twisted beyond recognition, the roar of the rockslide echoes nonstop in her head, and the longed-for angel of death is busy elsewhere. — A day like any other in as much as any day is the same as another and does not, upon closer inspection, turn out to be unique only minutes later when the present becomes the past. Or in hindsight. Looking back. At the film sequence playing henceforth on a huge screen before her eyes, one she can't stop imagining. At best she can tear it down and hide it from those whom she thinks haven't seen anything or weren't paying close attention. The rolled up, tattered celluloid strips within her will glow all the more brightly amidst the deepest darkness.

A day like any other in as much as the first

thing she did in the morning was open the French doors facing the garden and walk down the three steps. Standing now on the narrow gravel path leading around the rectangular lawn in the still-cool morning air of the first days of June, she pulled the belt of her floral-print robe tighter and briefly regretted having swapped the heavier lambskin-lined slippers for the lighter pink yarn ones with the flexible soles. The sight of the roses made her forget everything. Not just the shivering and that she had to ask her husband to bring up some wood for the fireplace in the evening and that she would take the 9:40 postbus to the local train station so she could go into the city. The roses returned her gaze with the expected shades of white to dark red. None of them had refused her. She thanked them for the early morning conversations of the last few months. There wasn't a day in late autumn, or the long winter, that passed without her stooping down to the plants, bending down to the frozen earth, to linger especially long at the rose bushes, speaking, without making a sound, to the future scent and petals. Besides the roses, there were the lavender, the phlox, the lupines, and the matthiolas. Before breakfast she made her daily round on the narrow gravel path, walking out to the thick hedges bordering the lawn and shielding the garden and back again to the French doors, and in the other direction to the bay laurel, the rhododendron, and the ivy. Here, there was a waist-high wall, behind which sheep were grazing. And suddenly his voice, like every morning, calling that the tea was ready.

*

In the French book *Une vie discrète*, there is a scene on page 64 that reminds her of another life. In a country house in Touraine, a father and his daughter stand facing each other in the parents' bedroom. She has come to say goodnight to him. In the adjoining bathroom accessed by a jib door, her mother is caring for her aging skin and pulling out the hair combs she uses during the day to put her hair up, which now falls in thinned-out strands over the collar of her pink nightgown. The father is standing in front of the drawn blue velvet curtains that reach all the way to the hardwood floor. He wants to go to bed soon, but he waits to undress. There is something he wishes to get off his chest. The bedspread, made of the same velvet as the curtains with an off-white lining, is already hanging on the arm of one of the three Louis XVI chairs. He lights his bedside lamp, and the white alabaster lampshade glows softly. Next to the gold alarm clock, there is a 700-page memoir, and on her mother's bedside table, The Life of Joan of Arc.

Father and daughter stand facing each other. She has been visiting her parents for a week, and she leaves tomorrow. Her father has been hoping that she would confide in him. Tell him about a love affair, or about a boyfriend for whom he would have nothing but contempt. He seems to hesitate, paces across the room, and stops at some distance from her. Looking away, he says abruptly, "Why are you being so opaque?" "And you?" she says in return. Offhandedly, jokingly. Instead his razor-sharp gaze, as if behind his pupils two blades were being sharpened. She is startled. Opaque. What does he want — that her body be made of glass? To look at the veins of her soul like the exhibits in his beloved museums, labelled, dated, November 5, 1968, a group of young people spending the evening sitting around a table in a fin-de-siècle coffeehouse, the eye contact, the ping-ponging of words exchanged over half-empty glasses, and the next day the rocky ride to Paris, rough bumps between buttocks and asphalt, driving through the outlying districts in the dark, the ever-increasing lights, the spotlights on the historic buildings, and finally turning into the narrow, barely lit dead-end street in the heart of the city. Hotel, nameless. Steep stairs up to an unlocked room. A sagging mattress. A night of passion. With whom? That is what he would like to know and not know. Would like to watch and turn away, filled with disgust. He had read and experienced enough.

What bothers him, the thorn in his side, is that he doesn't play a role in this drama. That his daughter does it without him, no matter what it is. That he remains outside this life. Like a dog that has to wait until his bowl is set in front of him, or he is offered a treat.

The gifts he gives his daughter are of the finest quality. Mohair, Shetland wool, silk. She puts them away and strokes them only in her thoughts. Patience is required, years and years of patience.

In the novel, the daughter exits the room and slams the door. She leaves the house and goes for a nighttime stroll. When she sees a shooting star in the sky, she forgets the wish she has been holding ready since the beginning of August. It is the 10th of the month. The other daughter has gone to bed with a book and doesn't fall asleep until morning. Pursued by those icy gray eyes.

*

Dream

The father is expected home. He is driving the car. It's getting dark. The family is still waiting on him. Slowly night falls. Something must have happened to him. He must have had an accident. No sign of life the whole night. Early the next morning — it's still dark — the daughter goes to the nearby train station consisting of a tiny lineman's shack with a bench in front. A black-shrouded figure sits there, huddled up. All that can be seen of this figure are the enormous dark eye sockets. Who is this? Is it death who has come to say that her father has met with an accident?

(After they moved to the country, he had talked about wanting to get a car.)

*

The couple has long since stopped living in this old spacious house, the husband is no longer working, and he has given up his small office in the city. Maintaining a double life has gotten difficult. She has finally called, taken out the slip of paper, dialed the number with the country code for Germany, and let it ring for a long time. Just as she is getting ready to hang up, she hears a clear, breathless voice: "Yes?" "Finally," says the voice, "I've been waiting a long time. He said you would call me one day." She is out of breath because she ran up the stairs. She had been outside in the garden reading one of his letters. "You're the great late love of my life. Infinitely tender but passionate, at the right moment. A wise, caring, and wonderfully sentimental woman: so mature, and yet so young. I bless the constellation that gave me the gift of you. Through you and with you I've regained my virile strength…." A small, enchanted, overgrown garden. She'll get to see it, sit in it, whereas he was never there, never entered her apartment in a former convent, doesn't know her home, and never glanced at her books, all four thousand of them. The woman talks and talks. Finally, someone is listening to her. She knows a lot about the much younger woman; she knows details about her life from his stories, his letters, hundreds of them back and forth. She has shared in all of it from afar.

A life lived at his side, invisible, always present. She waited for his call; she sat at home and waited and waited. And when the call came that he would be going alone to the doctor's the day after tomorrow between two and five o'clock in the afternoon, she boarded a train the next day and traveled seven hours to accompany him in a taxi and on foot, and afterward drink a cup of coffee and, after another farewell, ride back seven hours in the train, anxious and uncertain of whether she would ever see him again with her own eyes. This is the way it's been for years. What a life. Oh no, she sees it differently. She doesn't complain. She loves him, and she knows he loves her. That's enough for her. On that Monday at the end of May, two days before his birthday, he called and told her about his doctor's appointment. He hopes to see her, "I'm expecting you." Early in the morning she boarded the train, whereas he spent the night cramped in pain and sleepless, and the next day his bowels emptied themselves, his body pressing out everything going on inside him.

She waited at the appointed intersection, got into the taxi, and found him inside — weak, helpless, and at the mercy of old age like never before. He grabbed her hand, held it in his, and she wished the moment would last forever. Instead the taxi stopped shortly afterward in front of a gray, four-story townhouse where the doctor had his office. Leaning on her for support, the old man made it with difficulty to the second floor, where he was greeted by the doctor who had ordered bed rest and a strict diet for him. The same doctor, incidentally, who didn't give a thought to the old man's unknown companion, the woman he had never seen before, of whom he knew nothing, because it was part of his job to witness his patients' secrets, to hear them in sober sympathy, and to never act surprised. The taxi having waited in the meantime, they got back in again, and she road home with him. Like on the way there, he once again took her hand in his and held it tight.

She didn't board the train again the same day but instead traveled to an outlying district of the city where for years she had been renting a small one-room apartment, furnished with only the bare necessities, and waited — for what? She remembered how years ago she used to cook lunch on two hotplates, and when he showed up on time as usual at one o'clock, he would always joke, "I'm visiting you in your dorm room." They would eat lunch together at a table pushed up against the wall, laugh, express concern over a newspaper article, and exchange frequent glances full of happiness, melancholy, and love.

During the night she kept waking up, full of anxiety, and then fall back into a light sleep and restless dreams. In one of these dreams, the river with the reedy banks appeared, the one they had once strolled along together. With this lovely picture in mind, she was able to fall asleep again in the early morning hours, and now it was Wednesday, the day of his birthday, and she was sitting in her fleabag hotel, spending a never-ending day without the slightest sign of him, in the same city but continents apart. And never knowing if she'll ever see him again.

She talks and talks and finally someone is listening to her and taking an interest in her existence, remotely, secretly. At the same time, she is the center around which his thoughts revolve. When he is quiet, when he has that cool, reserved look on his face, when he must hide his overpowering desire, "… actually, I would like to wake up next to you every day, eat breakfast with you lightly dressed, and do much more…"

*

Dream

A couple is strolling through a meandering garden. It is summer. The couple saunters along, arm in arm, and stops once in a while to embrace. The woman is wearing white, and the man too is dressed in light colors. Suddenly the sky darkens. A strong wind kicks up, and the majestic old trees start to rustle furiously. The wood creaks and groans. The woman's light white dress billows up. While they stop once more to kiss a large branch crashes to the ground, right at the woman's feet. The couple falls silent, turns around, and runs back along the path that leads to an open summer house. Scarcely having made it inside, they hear a woman calling for the man with a loud and beseeching voice. She doesn't let the emerging storm stop her from wandering through the garden.

*

Who wouldn't want to reconcile the seemingly irreconcilable? Who wouldn't want, without having to lift a finger, to experience the resolution of these oppositions and differences in favor of benevolence and affection? What old, very aged man wouldn't be happy to experience how what was hidden can step into the light of day, how what has been secreted away can show itself under a bright sky, and how two women of different ages — whom he believed he had to keep away from each other and hide the existence of the one from the other, although both were close to him — can meet so he could live with the assurance that after his death his love would live on in the memories, conversations, and the communication between the two women? That's good, he apparently said, that's good. The women have seen photos of each other, and they are excited, curious, and open-minded.

They meet on the underground level of a train station exactly at the spot where the man used to stand when he picked up his children and later one of his grandchildren. It's a conspicuous location where you can't miss each other; where you can see the other person from a distance. Today it's the younger woman who watches the older one for a few minutes from afar. The woman is wearing a dark blue coat and a felt hat with an upturned brim offering a good look at a face that is still youthful, fair-skinned, and pretty. As she draws closer the younger woman sees the expression behind the blue-green glasses and now, at close range, the beautiful sparkling eyes. They walk towards each other, having recognized one another immediately. They move towards the exit of the concourse and choose a café where she has often sat with him. You should ask me some questions, says the older woman to the younger one. She is willing to answer anything, as well as she can. She doesn't put much stock in being secretive and doesn't want to hide anything. Everything about which she has hardly ever uttered a word should be brought out into the open.

How it began, the very first meeting, the moment in which sparks flew? At first, there was admiration for this educated, sensible, sober man and then — on excursions together and another time on a long stroll across the grass-covered hills until they could see the ocean at a distance — there developed a certain closeness, a rapport. The smile in those gray eyes of his watching the sheep graze as she raved about her favorite book. It's his, too. The first personal conversations. She shows her a photo from back then: how she is sitting next to him in a simple black dress with a round neckline, how their heads are leaning towards each other, how they are talking with each other. And how they have never stopped. For the last thirty-two years. Such a deep mutual understanding, such a natural closeness — he never knew that such closeness was possible between two people, such intimacy. He had never thought it possible for a man and woman to be so close. He had never known what affection was, all-embracing affection. It hit him like a wave — a wave of enveloping closeness and affection. He realized how lonely he had been.

*

The park and the palace where they had met. The meandering paths, the old trees. Near to the heath, the dunes, and the old city with the timber-framed houses. In this spacious wild park, the November storms had done their damage, uprooting and leveling trees, and the undergrowth was thick with ferns, butterbur, and belladonna growing hip high. And at the very back was the palace, long and gray, with its numerous chimneys, its rows of windows, and its elegant symmetry. After the war eminent figures of German and English nationality met here in a kind of higher institution for political and cultural exchange to bury the hostility, to communicate like human beings, like the bearers of culture, to prevent any future wars, and to develop appreciation and understanding.

The dark library with the green-hooded bankers' lamps and the deep silence. The large lounge with soft chairs placed around round tables, the heavy velvet curtains, the oil paintings of English landscapes, and the fireplace, smoldering during the day and blazing in the evening. She had attended his lecture on the previous evening and during tea she asked him, "May I?" She joined the man reading and told him how much she admired his wealth of knowledge. They talked every day for ten days in a row. Apparently he peppered her with questions about her work at the publishing house, about her life in Germany, about her Catholic childhood and youth, her education in Munich, her English studies, about her brief marriage to a soldier who fell at the front, and about her child that only lived one day. She had nothing to hide. He too. A large family, children long grown-up, a more than 30-year marriage, a fulfilled life. He described himself as happy. Later he will say, "I was incredibly lonely." Later. Back then they said farewell with the intention of never seeing one another again.

After a few months he wrote her. He couldn't and didn't want to live without this closeness, this intimacy, this love. For six years they felt completely free. Political conferences, historian gatherings — he often traveled alone. His wife didn't have any reason to be suspicious. Since she — sixteen years old, a beautiful, elegant girl, a classic beauty — walked into the new class, he had pursued her relentlessly. During the first lesson he kept turning around and staring at her with his gray-blue eyes. An early marriage, long stays abroad, a large family. He had matched the picture he drew of himself down to the last detail. The red-chalk drawing of the ten-year-old — upright forehead, straight nose, prominent chin — shows no trace of indecisiveness, of childlike chubbiness, of the playful, dreamy state of adolescence, a miniature man's head, close-cropped, looking towards the future without hesitation and reluctance, fearless and brave. This is how she knows him; to her, he is a rock. She is not surprised that Russian novels are his favorite books and Chopin his favorite composer.

And then this collapse of all certainties; the pride that disappears from his wife's eyes to be replaced by a helpless, insecure, at times pleading expression; and the sense of vertigo that accompanies the pain settling in. Advancing age has bent her back, caved in her chest, pushed her belly out, and lent her entire body an air of pitifulness. Her former sympathy for people and events seemed to have given way to a confused passivity, and the shock she had experienced — invisible to the outside world — was walled up inside her where no one would look, hidden and manifesting itself as pounding pain. No sooner had she opened her eyes than she awoke from a liberating dream. He hardly ever glanced at her with his dismissive, loveless eyes. Never an explanation, never a conversation. He didn't want to reveal anything. Instead he wrote his life down so people would believe him — a contribution to contemporary history.

Her own story doesn't appear in it at all. Upsetting and confusing and in no way like the image the former child had formed of himself at a time when others were wavering between sleep and dreams, between play and reality, between exuberance and sadness, and would continue for a long time to move, torn between zeal and apathy, on the now fragile ground of childhood and the unattainable heights on which adults seemed to walk around light-footed. The image of himself. It differs from another; it differs from the image the woman in the dark blue coat, at first in the coffeehouse and later in her small one-room apartment, paints of him in every detail — an affectionate, gentle, understanding person. Such that she is seized by a deep sadness never to have known such a father, but instead one who adamantly disapproved of her life, scornfully referred to her friends as bums, and never understood her sense of independence. Much later a closeness and understanding came about, by way of books, writing, and probably through the influence of this woman sitting across from her talking about him and their time together in this small apartment where she cooked for him, where they ate, held conversations, and made love. The older woman having taken off her hat, the younger one now sees her high forehead, small nose, and pretty mouth. Her ageless face illuminated as if by an invisible light. She, the daughter, understands the man. She will tell him. She wished he would have started a new life with this woman. Sometimes they had imagined what it would have been like if they had moved to England and lived in a small cottage. She wouldn't have begrudged the lovers their happiness. She would have understood it and been happy about it. Why hadn't he had the courage?

*

One year before his death, father and daughter will have a talk. She couldn't bear the thought of him dying without having had the chance to ask him her questions, and what she heard were his evasive, empty answers and the word "discretion" over and over again. Padded walls and doors, nothing that could leak out. The only thing he regrets is that he hadn't been able to maintain discretion.

*

A discrete life. A quiet, reserved appearance. Loneliness, perhaps. To the outside world, silent, unspectacular, and enigmatic. A private life of which nothing leaks out. Shut off from all curiosity. Quiet, calm, almost unnoticeable. Here, however, in this discrete life, the peace and quiet turn into a muffled silence between high rooms, caught in velvet curtains. Voices suddenly falling silent, and the pleading eyes of the one person meeting the dismissive eyes of the other. A postbox address in the city, hidden letters — none could be found after his death. And the three shrill rings of the telephone in the long hallway of a big old house. Absence, although the body, the mind is present. Inexplicable coldness and a complete refusal to discuss things. "Une vie discrète," a gray veil of silence entangling unanswered questions that never go away. A secret that will be taken to the grave.

*

The daughter looks down at the foot as it fumbles for a slipper, stares at the blue-veined skin on the surface, at the purple spots that look like a lake undergrown with algae in the blue-red light of the setting sun, stares at the colors, at the hunk of flesh, at the big toe — a yellowed, ivory-colored, skin-covered fossil — sees the foot feel its way across the gray carpet for a leather sandal, while the other leg, the other foot, hang halfway over the edge of the bed, lifeless. They must belong to an old man despite the writing utensils, the numerous newspapers — read and taken apart — scattered across the duvet, and the stack of books in English, German, and French on the antique nightstand. A still-alert mind in this finely shaped skull, a model for sculptors and painters, even as a child. Photographed countless times and always the two contradictory expressions of his eyes: in one picture, a soft, material gray with a blue shimmer, and in the next one, taken a little later, a stony gray. And the change is always unexpected and startling for the person on whom the gaze falls. After more than sixty years, the woman at his side still can't stand it, particularly since she has been receiving the dismissive look more and more often in recent years without any apparent reason.

She checks the clock to see whether it's time to eat soon. She is expecting her son who is going to take her out to a nearby restaurant. She looks in the mirror at the gray-blue silk blouse, the blue necklace, her white hair. After his foot, still naked and unslippered, finally rests on the floor, the old man, in his loose-fitting striped pajamas with the top mother-of-pearl button open, exposing his mother-of-pearl chest hair — its white slightly discolored by the gray-pink skin showing through — reaches with his youthful-looking hand for his glasses, which have slid from the pillow down to the sheet, and delves again into his birthday mail — a few letters and a telegram — after last year receiving countless letters and his picture with an article in the daily newspapers (as again later after his death). He has laid down again, closed his eyes, and then afterward throws back the comforter and says he feels far too weak to get dressed and go out to eat. She replies that she will accompany him to the dining room and eat with him. With her arm for support, he will slowly inch forward, step by step, in his belt-tied dressing gown, and they will sit at a table for two with a view of the flower beds and the flourishing shrubs, and he will order white wine and talk about the past when he stayed as a guest at one of the country estates on Lake Neuchâtel, on Lake Geneva, friends with the host, and he will reminisce about the gardens decorated with boxwoods and roses, about an open colonnade, about the view of the vineyards, and the blue of the lake. After that, he will sit there in silence, lost in his thoughts, picturing the people for whom he longs. Bidding the other diners goodbye as they leave the dining room together, they will return to their senior apartment, and he will lie down and fall asleep before their son, who traveled there by train, will enter with his innate liveliness, hug his sleeping father, accompany his mother to the restaurant, and encourage her to order whatever her heart desires. She will sit there before the expensive fish dinner with drooping shoulders and an insatiable desire for an all-encompassing sense of satiety that this dish, this sautéed pike-perch fillet and the much-anticipated strawberry mousse for dessert, cannot give her; nor her son's stories, his chattiness, and his radiance, which is nothing more than a distant reflection of the light that radiated from him in his early years when the happy child frequently served as a mirror for his mother. The old woman pokes at her fish while her husband is at home fast asleep under the gray-blue comforter.

She looks at the man sleeping there — one blue-veined hand lying on the comforter — how he breathes easily, free of pain, and she sees a vast sky and remembers how her father used to be, his razor-edged words, "what's this for a bum you've dug up again. You'll have to lie in the bed you've made." The sharp-sighted father had recognized the couple walking close together as they left the shadows and stepped into the light flooding the square in front of the arcades. The father tried to shake off this annoying image. Why couldn't his daughter choose a young man in this sedate town from a well-known family, from decent stock, a respectable person? Why must she always fall for these total strangers whom her father feared like the plague? Just as strange as the boyfriends were later the rooms in which they lived, which didn't correspond in the least with what a caring father would wish for his daughter: attic apartments under scorching roofs and ground-level garden apartments with head-high weeds growing in front of the windows. Where did this love of — or better yet — addiction to these kinds of dwellings come from? Dwellings in which she led a life her father couldn't bear to see, one that scared him, as if he didn't already have his hands full with his own life, with its dark sides, which were at the same time the brightest and most colorful. While his daughter took the liberty of doing what she felt was right for all to see and was ready to pay the price, he, on the other hand, kept all the rebelliousness, the splendid non-conformity of his younger years under lock and key, sealed away behind a double-plated iron door, never to see the light of day again. He had worked hard to construct his visible life, and once properly supported, it was supposed to run its course. But things had turned out quite differently. What this must have meant to him, this crumbling of walls, this unexpected light, this passion which sparked to life in a beautiful, faraway place in a foreign land under a different sky.

She is still looking at her sleeping father when her mother and brother return. Afterward her brother accompanies her to the bus stop and hands her a slip of paper with an address and a telephone number. He tells her that her father said she could contact the woman. She thanks him and returns home completely unaware of a room — a simple room not so far away — where the unknown woman sits, worries, maybe even cries, and after a day of futile waiting on her part, will board a train and ride the seven hours home.

*

On the train ride home, images from the depths of her childhood surface against the backdrop of the landscape as if her unconscious were seeking the inviolable, a happiness not darkened by shadow. Children need these images when they think of their fathers and mothers. Adults also tend to gild their memories until they learn better. Yet the images hang there even if afterward they are cast in a different light. The former child will try to hold on to them no matter what happened afterward, no matter what unforeseeable turn events took. The colors of these early images shine brightly, and the outlines emerge clearly. Images in which father and mother appear as one, as if sitting high on a throne, a couple that retreated to the glass-covered veranda after lunch every day to drink a small cup of coffee, moments of intimacy from which the children were excluded, where the two sat next to each other on a striped couch in private conversation, sipping every now and then from their cups, undisturbed, insulated, two people in love. The small bedroom they shared for years also kindled the imagination of children who knew nothing about the making of children; it was a windowless, cell-like room with two antique beds, above which hung a gold-framed painting by Benozzo Gozzoli depicting princes and horses, and a door which was closed during the night and from which they left their child-free realm in the morning with a smile on their face.

And how back then he gave her the jewelry in such a way that she seemed suddenly surrounded by a golden halo when she untied the small white package, opened the emerald-green suede case with the apricot silk lining, and took the gold necklace out of it. He placed it around her neck — he, who never had a cent to spare, who had saved, taken on an extra job, had to work nights — and how she looked at him, and the children stood by and gazed in wonder, ran their fingers along the soft leather case, felt the silk lining, and how she kept her first gold necklace on all evening and he — proud.

And the summer holidays in a certain year that, like rays of sunshine, cast a glow over her childhood: the holidays at the lake, the swimming, the boat rowing, the heat, the light clothes, father without his tie, mother with bare legs, and the days vast and sprawling. Once, on a cliff overlooking a large Jurassic lake where they were all sitting together, mother began to speak — somewhat solemnly, somewhat cautiously and measuredly, keeping her eyes focused on the surface of the lake — and announced that the three children would be getting a new sibling, a child would be born next spring, which meant that their parents loved each other, that the family was an inviolable unit, a realm within the world where everything had its proper place, where there was no doubt and uncertainty, where one was safe as long as one remained an obedient child and couldn't imagine things being any other way. Only much later did the questions begin to arise, the doubt, the rebellion, and much later still, the cracks, the fissures, the swaying ground beneath one's feet.

*

A silken sky outside, cloudless, and the sleeping old man, half covered, the pile of books on his bedside table, his pipe and matches on a squat table; ever since she was a child, newspapers and tobacco crumbs have littered the floor, the familiar sight of father's things. Next door her mother is fiddling around, bent over, talking to her brother who is going to accompany her to the bus. She casts another glance at her sleeping father, his almost youthful face. The shape of his body is visible under the blanket: his powerless, frail body; his legs that can barely support him; and his crooked violet-blue feet that cause him to fall every few days, making him reliant on help. He dare not go out on his own, completely dependent now physically on someone accompanying him, while his alert mind reads and writes in three different languages and takes part in a world he shall soon leave, a world from which he is ready to depart. And he has never said a word about how he imagines an afterwards, or if he even believes in an afterwards, a life after death. He has never engaged in such speculations; he wants to be cremated and have his ashes scattered in the river he used to play in when he was a boy. Nothing should remain — no grave decorated with flowers, no place to remember him. Some years ago he said that the few people who come together after his death should sing the song that goes "ce n'est pas un adieu mes frères, ce n'est qu'un au-revoir," meaning he would see the people dear to him once again. Mother, on the other hand, wants to be buried in a cemetery so they would be separated in death: she in a grave crowned with roses, and he as ashes in the river, ultimately in the ocean. And the word soul has rarely ever crossed his lips, perhaps set aside in an earlier circle of friends, finally at its place of destination, wherever that may be, free.

*

Who could recognize in this reclining, sleeping old man — ready to strip off his mortal shell — who could recognize in him the young boy wearing the military cap in the black-and-white photo, or the boy in the red chalk drawing — gazing into the future — who could recognize the sleeping old man in this boyish face striving for independence? He has fallen yet again: he falls several times a day now, his legs can no longer support him, he suddenly finds himself on the floor. He doesn't go anywhere anymore. He sits on the balcony where he reads, writes, and thinks about his life. He still knows some details of his childhood. He remembers his elementary school teacher whom he loved. He remembers his schoolmates and can rattle off their names. He remembers the day the new girl joined the class, blushing; he remembers this beautiful, noble-looking girl, a classic beauty. He remembers the early days of his marriage with her, his longing for big cities, and his life abroad. He remembers his long military service and his fear for his family, whom he had sent to the countryside. He remembers his friends, who are all dead now, especially the one in whom he confided, who understood him, who was discreet and would take what he knew with him to the grave. He remembers the postwar years, the cities in ruins, and his fallen friends. He remembers his trip to England and his encounter with a foreign woman as if he had always been waiting for her. Was it in summer or in fall?

*

His daughter is now the same age as he was when they met in that spacious seventeenth-cen-

71

tury palace; when their love began, and they strolled through the park together. This is where their love originated, in this beautiful place they journeyed to from different countries so their paths would cross. She would like to know how this first meeting took place. Were they sitting at neighboring tables at dinner, or did they have tea next to each other in front of the large fireplace, or were they walking towards each other down a long hallway, or did their paths cross on a morning walk? She had wanted to ask him about this and many other things, but now it's too late. She will have to live with this sorrow and imagine it all for herself, see it all in her mind's eye. At this point, she still doesn't know the woman who will tell her; she still doesn't know anything.

And how must he have felt when they, his wife and he, years later rented a house in the country, fulfilled their dream, and shortly after the move, his wife had found the letter in the drawer of his dingy desk in the tiny office he rented in the city, and the shadows of his secret life spread throughout that gorgeous country home? This is where, at first vaguely, the headaches had begun, a mild dizziness initially. This is where the telephone rang in the long hallway.

This is where he telephoned as soon as her mother went into town to do the shopping. This where the reality of life contrasted with the ideal place. This is where her father increasingly developed that icy gray look in his eyes. This is where he began to write his memoirs and to paint an image of himself for posterity that they should take for the real one, the uncontested picture of an honest man beyond reproach. The same picture captured in the red chalk drawing of 1918 depicting the young boy gazing courageously into the future. Nothing dreamy in that face, nothing undecided, uncertain, and this is how his life should continue without detours or wrong turns. He should forge ahead, always moving in the right direction, always standing on the right side, where others, fickle and cowardly, conformed during the war years. A fearless, difficult fellow, he worked on his memoirs while she, his wife, went knocking at the doors of the farmers' wives, sat in their big kitchens, listened to them complain about their oldest son or weather-related ailments, about the hail two weeks ago, while she waited for beans, tomatoes, and carrots, carried them home, and then wondered why his eyes were absent and cold.

It was the house of both of their dreams, a country house like in a nineteenth-century novel, a garden on each side, large square rooms, wood-paneled. One simply had to be happy here.

And when the one daughter came for a visit, she was overcome with a vague anxiety she couldn't explain; an impenetrable silence hung in the bright rooms like a dark cloth. If it hadn't have been for the lake — this nearby moor lake with the reed-lined shore and the water lilies, this charming lake nestled into the countryside and surrounded by corn fields where the husband swam his daily laps until the weather turned cool in fall — the situation might have come to a head, there might have been some drama, a tragedy, like in a nineteenth-century novel, if it weren't for the lake with its soft moor water, the clouds reflecting on its surface, and the waterfowl. Then, in the evening, the renewed silence, her mother's inexplicable sighs, and her father's brusqueness. She, the daughter, didn't say a word about her life. There was nothing to tell that would have pleased her father, and then one evening, the words, the reproach, she is opaque, this unforgettable scene, her reply, wasn't he rather opaque too, and his face, which closed up, his scrutinizing eyes. No, she didn't know anything. Her father denied her his story. She didn't know why they had never felt comfortable in that wonderful house, not one single hour.

She is now the same age as he was back then when he met her, and she wonders what event in her life will happen so totally unexpectedly, without warning. She wonders how it must have been for him back then to be thrown off track. Perhaps he had been scared, perhaps he had met the unknown within himself for the first time, and this must have been quite a shock for someone at such an advanced age, to discover that one is completely at the mercy of one's feelings. And, at the same time, this feeling of joy like none he had ever known before.

*

To talk with him. To break the silence, just once. There was this one hour back then, a bright, quiet hour. He was lying in his hospital bed, weak, but in good spirits. He had slept, read, and before him was the broad window and beyond that the backdrop of the city. On the other side of the river, whose depths remained hidden, there was a long row of old houses built side by side with mansard roofs, and behind the houses, the Tower of Münster, which one could walk up, past an apartment halfway up — as a child he wished to live there, to be the watchmen's son — and beyond Münster, the hill, partially forested, and above, the wide open sky, a marvelous view. He lay there in bed in calm spirits; no one else was in the room. Now was her chance to speak with him — the words formed behind her lips but remained stuck there in finished sentences. She thought of nothing else while they traded benign words. There would never be another opportunity to be alone with him like now behind this double door, where nobody could hear the loudly spoken words, for he was hard of hearing, and she kept looking at his still handsome face to see if she could detect a sign of willingness to reveal something about himself, but she couldn't notice anything, nothing except the relaxed expression of a convalescent patient, and while the time ticked away she knew she would walk away empty-handed, back through the labyrinthine corridors to the hospital exit without learning anything about him, without knowing what was going on inside him.

*

She remembers a day at the end of May, years ago. Hazy heat, drowsy, and conciliatory too. The train ride there — the framed pictures of a landscape that looked different each time she glanced out the window. A blue-white shimmer that brought out the brilliance of the colors, highlighting their intensity as if from a deeper layer. The same sky, the hazy light unchanging throughout the long afternoon, and conciliatory thoughts that accompanied her on the trip to the two aged persons, to her parents, to conversations, to a conversation on a walk, step by step, word for word. Her anticipation, her suspense. A secret was going to be revealed, laid out before her in all its uniqueness. Her father and her had planned the walk, just the two of them. It had been his idea: he had chosen a path that was too difficult for her mother. They wanted to stroll along the river for hours, the river of his childhood, in which he had plunged as a boy and then later as a young man and even later as an old man, the river with the strong current. They wanted to stroll along the bank for a long time. He wanted to talk with her, had planned the walk, and as they stood in the door ready to go, her mother had slipped on her coat and accompanied them as if she had sensed that father and daughter were going to share a secret, as if she were afraid to leave the two of them alone, as if she were scared of an intimacy that could develop on the walk. It was a magnificent, mild May day. She remembers her sadness, her disappointment, and her dwindling hope for just such a chance, for a togetherness, for a conversation that was never going to happen, not even now in the hospital room in which he can probably call every day, undisturbed, there, far away, where a woman lives that he has never stopped loving.

*

She talks about it on the phone. How she traveled there, the day before, seven hours long, and they rode together to the doctor's in a taxi. Afterward they went together to a café where you couldn't hear yourself speak. Outside on the sidewalk they were tearing up the pavement, jackhammers pounding away, and therefore their conversation was limited to just a few words and lots of silent gestures and meaningful looks. Every time, she tries to burn the image of his face into her memory, never knowing when and if she will ever see him again. The next day another opportunity presented itself for them to meet. They sat together for a long time in the garden of the retirement home. He was in good spirits, rosy and lively, and he wore a light-colored linen jacket and smoked his pipe. This is how she photographed him — one of the last pictures — and afterward they had drunk coffee in the cafeteria. It didn't seem to bother him to be seen with her there; he seemed to ignore the looks his fellow residents gave him. In these moments, he only had eyes for her and wondered when they would see each other again. And the next day, the long trip again. She has to make do with these few hours. This has been her life for decades, and why get worked up about it. One is willing to do anything for a great love, and as long as he loves her, as long as his feelings for her remain unchanged, as long as he asks her not to leave him and to take advantage of every opportunity to see him, to be together — yes, this has been her life for decades, and she doesn't know any other. "It's how it is."

*

Seven hours in the train, and days full of longing, inner tension, and anticipation: all this to see him perhaps for just one single hour, to sit somewhere, hold his hand, while time slips away and one minute after the other vanishes forever — is this what love looks like, the everlasting, never-ending kind? So much devotion, so much selflessness, such a deep bond between an old and a very aged person. May the day be beautiful; may the sky be clear; may the father, leaning on her arm, be able to walk, to move; may their time together take place under a lucky star; may it not be their last farewell; and may that final day be postponed into the indefinite future.

*

How they loved their gardens. There were many of them. One was large and intricate, with a meadow full of dandelions in the back and lines stretched on poles to hang up the laundry.

There the garden was sunny and treeless, while the rest was shady and dark. A narrow gravel path lined with boxwoods led from the meadow to a tuff grotto, above which a chestnut tree spread out its branches. On the other side of the fence, in the neighbor's yard, a golden ball glinted in the sun, and a group of deer paused, remarkably lifelike. From the grotto one came to another yard, in front of the house, and on the façade, under the windows, bloomed roses and lilies, her favorite flower, and in fall, dahlias in their vibrant colors. On one side of the house, there grew a tall walnut tree which cast a shadow on another part of the yard where the children played and quarreled in the afternoon. A further garden was laid out terrace-like above the river flowing deep down below. There she had let the roses grow on arches to form bright arbors and to the side stood an old ivy-covered garden house where she played with her first grandchild. The prettiest garden, though, was located at the back of the country house which they had been fortunate enough to rent, thus fulfilling one of their dreams, the house in which so much silence, so many unspoken words, and such a great, dull sadness filled the space between the rooms, and where the long telephone calls took place in the hallway as soon as she went to town to do the shopping. There, behind the house, surrounded on three sides by tall shrubs, was the most beautiful of all the gardens, her oasis of happiness, of unhappiness, where she went first thing in the morning, bent down to the flowers — mallows, roses, matthiolas, larkspurs, and lupines — where she stepped from one flower to the next in the floral print robe which she often kept on for hours in the morning the older she got. She gave the flowers her full attention, all her love, and she held conversations with them, for which they thanked her. This Eden-like garden was the first place she went in the morning and the last place before she went to bed. Through the bushes the rural sounds of the village could be heard: wagon wheels, a hay blower, boys' voices, the bells of cows returning home, and their dull steps. She sat here alone for hours, reflected on her life, sought a deeper meaning in the letter she had found, a love letter, written in a different garden, a small green oasis with herbs, weeds, flowers, and tall reeds, at the very back of which flourished shrubs, as high as the house, and there was an old sunshade and a striped garden chair where the other woman sits, reads, and writes, maybe to him, here in her favorite place, in this small wild garden that he never saw and never will see.

*

Also in the novel *Une vie discrete*, Madame has a garden in Tours. It's a long rectangle running along the entire backside of the house. In the middle of the lawn, there is a circular flower bed. The gardener comes once a month. Madame doesn't have a particular relationship with her garden. She looks indifferently at the green all around, happy that it puts some distance between her house and that of her neighbor who she has never really liked. Is Madame bored? Not at all. She embroiders pictures, masterpieces from the Louvre Museum. And she watches TV. Sex and crime. She doesn't miss her husband. Every morning she goes to the "Aux trois Voûtes" coffeehouse, resplendently furbished in shades of red and gold. Every day an elderly man sits there, alone. One day they start talking and become friends. The coffeehouse is where they meet. A few tendernesses, pleasant conversations — the 70-year-olds don't want more than that.

Paris, Rue Victor Cousin. Is that Monsieur Professor coming out of the house, looking up at the cloudy sky, hesitating, and then walking away rapidly despite the heavy black leather case in his right hand? He won't reappear until evening and vanish into the house. Shortly afterward a woman with blond hair, lots of make-up, gold-rimmed glasses, and a face no longer young will enter the house. One and a half hours later, the couple is sitting in a brasserie having dinner. At around 11 o'clock, the couple walks back to the house, arm in arm. On the next day, the professor meets one of his daughters for lunch. His difficult daughter, as he used to call her. In the meantime, he has confided in her and since then their relationship has been friendly and respectful. The daughter is wearing one of her father's previous gifts, the soft mohair scarf from a shop in London.

Une vie discrète, set between Paris and Tours, moves away from her own story, is no longer similar, only remotely, when it describes how the professor confides in his children, the one son on a long hike in Brittany, near the Atlantic, under a vast gray sky with squawking seagulls flying overhead. How the son nods understandingly, wants to meet the woman whom he will later visit several times, and how he can finally tell his father about his relationships with men, which brings them closer together than ever before. Whereas in her own story, it was a wide, gently sloping alpine pasture where father and son talked. The father spoke of how he met her, his love, and how much he wants him to meet the woman, how he finally wanted to get something off his chest that had been plaguing him for a long time, and this son too will understand him and not be surprised by his father's love. Later, in another year, on another continent, the father will confide in his eldest daughter. Here, once again, on a hike along the ocean, as if the vast surface of the water, a lofty sky, the even pace of their steps, would set the words free from within him, where he doesn't have to look the other person in the face, where he could gaze at the choppy sea and a sailboat in the distance, and as if talking to himself get off his chest what has been plaguing him, and this daughter too will understand him and not show her astonishment. The two younger daughters are the only ones who will learn about their father's secret love from someone other than him, which they will never get over, too much had they wished to have a private conversation with their father, the face-to-face talk that her father had feared. In the end all of the children will know, and, what the father would have never hoped to expect, they will understand and approve of it as if they were relieved to discover the human weaknesses of their father. A father who finally steps down from his imaginary pedestal and disappears, without a sound, into the anonymous crowd of unfaithful men.

*

The picture. The top is taken up by a bright cloudless sky. Swallows dart back and forth. Beneath that, a table, a pastel tablecloth, in front of a balcony balustrade. On both sides, the gray concrete walls. At the table, a man and a woman sit across from each other. Their upper bodies are leaning in toward each other. Closeness. The man's hair is white, and his skin is that of a very aged man. The woman is also no longer young. She looks at him with inexpressible tenderness. They drink coffee. They talk. Nobody can hear what they are saying. Sometimes their heads move close together, or their hands seek each other on the tablecloth. It is a peaceful image that recurs across the whole world, always the same. Two people at a table, affection between them. Love. They sit there that way for a long time. An entire afternoon. The afternoon is given them as a gift, and they accept it with gratitude. They don't know when they will get another afternoon together like this. They can't choose themselves. As soon as an opportunity presents itself, the one person hurries to the other. It's the woman. The man can no longer travel, get around, hop on board, hop off, cross streets, and climb stairs. He must wait until he is blessed with a new rendezvous by those who act for him, who are able to take matters into their own hands. Summer isn't over yet, and there is still a chance of the picture repeating itself, under a bright cloudless sky, the swallows darting around with their white rump feathers. They don't know if they will ever see each other again. The view from afar, two people on a balcony on a clear summer day.

*

The husband in the story *Une vie discrete* is a historian. He has to travel regularly from Tours to Paris, where he works in archives and libraries. He has had an attic apartment in the Rue Victor Cousin for some time. There, he meets his lover, who travels from Brussels. She can be in Paris in a few hours. His wife has no reason to be suspicious. A historian who needs more than a day to research certain questions. What she can't fail to notice is the obvious good mood he is in when he returns from Paris, whereas otherwise, he is rather reserved, sometimes even dismissive. She attributes it to the fact that he must have found what he was looking for or made a new discovery.

Madame is satisfied with her life. She doesn't miss being close to her husband who otherwise is an attentive, caring husband, who always brings her back pralines from her favorite confectionary in Paris, and from time to time, at irregular intervals, takes her to the Opéra, after which they always stay in the same hotel. Madame has her friends in Tours, her quiet life, her coffeehouse friend, and her television shows.

*

Whereas here, in her story, things have gotten difficult for the two lovers. They never know when they'll see each other again, and they don't know if each meeting will be their last. They mourn and bid farewell to their short time spent together. His 91st birthday today. His wife, whose head hurts so bad it feels like it's going to explode, who talks about how well her children have turned out, about her long, happy marriage while casting an insecure look at her one daughter who says nothing and keeps her thoughts to herself, for a long time now, and her husband in his dressing gown, lifting a cup of tea to his mouth with hands that seem delicate and arouse feelings of tenderness, with his distinctive head, narrower now than ever before but still reminiscent of the bust of him as a young man, the one that conceals his look, the gentle-hearted, serious, gray-blue one, and the stony, cool, unforgiving one. The always vigilant eyes whose attention has started to wane only recently, lost in reverie, perhaps gazing there where she, his lover, lives in her apartment surrounded by books and sometimes sits in the wilderness of her small garden where he has never been, in that place he has never sought except in his thoughts, where he may be at that moment or somewhere else entirely, though he is sitting in the living room surrounded by his daughter and his wife, he, the old man, waiting for his son, his youngest daughter, the oldest granddaughter, and her daughter, his great-granddaughter, he sits there, speechless, not reading, not watching TV, just staring into an unknown distance, into himself, and the question arises: who is there, who?

Which is why his wife suddenly stands up and kisses him, with an almost defiant pride; why she demonstratively, even possessively grabs his head and presses her mouth on his at precisely the moment when his granddaughter presses the shutter button, or conversely, asks her granddaughter to photograph her at this moment, a document that will outlive her, a piece of evidence whose effect won't be lost on the descendants who will look at it someday, a long-lasting marriage, a unique love. The one granddaughter and her younger brother look at the picture with satisfaction, pride; their mother looks at it over their heads, she understands the old woman, the aged mother, who lets herself be photographed in this way, who shows herself in the right light, an uprising before the imminent end.

She is holding his head: of him all one can see is a tuft of white hair, part of a face with brown liver spots, and a neck of wrinkled skin with her arm slung around it, her head bending down, and of her the back of her head — bald patches showing through her white hair — her dangling necklace, and, although neither her mouth nor his can be seen, it is clear that she is kissing him right on the mouth. Someday the picture will be pasted into an album, looked at, and talked about. It has a certain immortality in contrast to the two people kissing, whereas no picture of the other woman exists, nowhere; she will disappear into her shadowy existence as if she had never existed. After he is dead, where is the evidence that she ever existed, who will keep her memory, remember her?

*

Dream

A wide, slow-flowing river spanned by a bridge with an ornate iron railing. On one side of the bridge, a stone statue of Mary rises up in the middle of the balustrade. The river and the bridge traverse a town. It is late afternoon, quitting time. A densely packed crowd crosses the bridge moving in both directions. On one end of the bridge stands the woman, the lover, dressed in light colors, and on the other, the man in a dark hat and coat. They try to reach each other but are repeatedly driven back by the crowd. They can't move an inch forward, and the distance between them remains the same. It is a desperate, futile attempt to come together. The stream of people doesn't let up. The light and dark figures at each end of the bridge seem to be rooted to the spot. Unmoved, the stony face of Mary looks down on them. She has his wife's features. End of May, beginning of June, a bright bygone time. Now is November, All Souls' Day. Parting hangs in the air like a wind-torn spider web glinting in the rays of the November sun.

*

She is sitting on a bench under the falling leaves and waiting amidst the piles of autumn foliage to see if he will come, which isn't certain. She waits and hopes and listens. Was that a rustling I heard? Was that the sound of steps? She won't stop hoping that he will appear shortly, stand before her, so they can walk arm in arm up and down this long avenue, between the trees losing their leaves, their yellow-brown leaves. She hopes, waits, and only after a full hour does she get up, suddenly aged, and slowly walk away, constantly looking back to see his likeness appear among the trees in a dark winter coat — which he has been wearing recently — a dark arm raised high, waving. She turns her head back and looks again, one last time.

*

One last picture. The oval shape of the mirror reflects their heads: the head of the old woman and that of the old man, facing each other, leaning in toward each other, the gold frame of the mirror enclosing an image of a long familiarity, intimacy, togetherness, and beyond the frame, nothing visible, nothing tangible, nothing. Back to the beginning — the faces old, the hair white — back to where their faces first turned toward each other and touched, like now in the gold-framed mirror, and everything in between erased, invisible, lost in the shadow of time.

II.

No, as if providence itself had intervened. This great love was not meant to vanish into nothing, nor fall victim to eternal silence. It was to be given the chance to flare up once again, late, very late. A few months before his death, as it were, he became dependent on nursing care. That which is normally feared was regarded as a great stroke of luck, as a late present. And as chance, fate, or whatever would have it, the nursing ward in the retirement home where he lived with his wife was overcrowded, and thus no bed was available for him. He would have to find a bed elsewhere in the nursing ward of a beautiful baroque retirement home in the city center. A magnificent building with a large inner courtyard and a splashing fountain. From time to time the large shiny black car drives into the grassy courtyard and collects a corpse. The old people sitting there watch the scene unfold with a mix of curiosity and satisfaction. Their hour has yet to come, although no resident has ever left the home alive. The floors of the building have long, dim hallways and wide alcoves with tables and chairs in front. This is where the old people — or one is tempted to say, inmates — sit. For many of them are unresponsive; others sit around the whole day in stubborn silence; and some make incomprehensible sounds and let out short, high-pitched screams. A small white-haired woman, lost in her own world, cries repeatedly for her mother, transformed once again into a small helpless child. Here, at one of these tables, the man will spend his remaining time on earth, his eyes gazing down on the open newspaper, a dead pipe in his mouth. His lover sits with him day after day. She peels him an orange, feeds him grapes, and holds his hand. And keeps a journal. In the evening she writes down the short dialogues in a notebook. Here, they finally belong together and can be a couple. His own wife only visits him briefly and not even every day. It's easy to see her coming down the long corridor as if in a hurry, and that's when the lover and girlfriend leaves her seat, knowing she will return soon. The wife never stays longer than a quarter of an hour. She sits briefly with her husband, listens to his confused words, and lacks the patience to wait until he speaks one clear, coherent sentence. She will never consider what he says to be anything other than an incomprehensible string of indistinct words. In an act of triumph, she will speak of him as feeble-minded. (He who once possessed a sharp mind and infallible judgment). His girlfriend sees him quite differently. She waits patiently and listens attentively until he forms words into what will be his last sentences. A simple everyday conversation at the end of a lifetime. Precious final words.

She wrote down the following:

"It seems to me as if I've lived another life." — "You've lived a good, full life."

"It's wonderful that you're here."

"It's a shame I can't offer you anything here."

He feeds me and lets me drink from his cup.

"I feel like I've aged fifty years."

"I'm no longer the man I used to be." — "You still have the same handsome head and distinctive face."

"Are you bored?" — "Not in the least. And you?" — "I'm never bored, not the least when you're here."

I must go back to Germany from time to time, and when I return: "Where were you so long? High time you put in an appearance."

"Do you still like me?" — "I'll always like you."

"Where are you going?" — "Home, to the tiny apartment where you were often." — "Ah, so often. It was nice."

He can still read. He is obsessed by a place in a book where his name is mentioned. "I never knew he mentioned me."

He still reads several newspapers.

He speaks a lot, but inarticulately.

What he mainly wants, though, is tenderness and affection.

"One has to know me well not to fly into a rage. I'm an intolerable pain in the ass."

When I return from Germany: "It's great you could manage it again, darling. I'm happy."

"Sometimes one is tired although one hasn't done anything…" — "You've done more than enough in your life…" – "And everything always so fast."

Then he is lost in his thoughts.

"What will the world look like in 200 years? Perhaps they'll have invented…"

"My dearest companion through all these years, thank you for your great patience…"

"I must be sure that I'll find you again…"

"Your love is overwhelming…"

He speaks about wanting to visit a green idyll in the countryside. "When are we leaving this building?"

"You aren't allowed to leave…" — "No, I'm not leaving."

Then he says quite clearly: "I thank you for everything, my darling." His very last words. Afterward, silent caresses and touches. Kissing and holding hands.

At 10 p.m. on the same day, he passes away. In the evening I return and sit with my dead lover. Gaze at his handsome, suddenly youthful face. Remain a long time sitting there, a very long time, a silent goodbye. Until, long after midnight, the door opens quietly, and a nurse gently sees me out.

III.

"Zur Stund" is the name of the house in a sleepy lane — enveloped still in morning's silence — in which a friend of hers lives, a friend she has confided in. She sleeps in the attic apartment of the old house and knows nothing about today's trip, about setting forth from "zur Stund," the beginning of a process — starting right this hour — of verifying a reality internalized long ago, or about the visit that will begin with this train ride. The visit to an old lady: it's not a comedy, even less a tragedy, no literary genre whatsoever. Rather, it's a slice of a life story, the unknown, hidden part of the life of a woman and a man who loved each other.

The previous nights' dreams were uneasy,

her sleep fragmented, her drowsy waking up to the electronic ring of the alarm clock reluctant, and the day before not spent "in great anticipation," as the old woman said of herself, but in great distress. And now, right beside the tracks, separated only by a swath of grass and old trees, the vast surface of the lake, gray and choppy, under a cloudy sky. The masts of the sailboats swaying in the bays. And across from her they're talking about the waxing and the waning of the moon. Later, the motionless deer over there, on the edge of the woods, evocative of her childhood — the grazing deer in the neighbor's yard never moved a muscle back then, and for a long time the child wasn't sure if it was alive or merely a lawn decoration, which in her mind has always lent the deer an air of the fabulous, as if it were the enchanted girl in that old French song who is killed by her brother during a hunt and begins to speak that evening, served on a silver platter — the deer in the neighbor's yard next to that old, shady house in which the family lived, the three children, the still young father, and the charming, loving mother, the memory of the parents sitting next to each other, each with a demitasse in front of them, after lunch, their conversation undisturbed, oblivious to the children, back then, in the safety of one's own little world, despite the war, an oasis of bliss, a half-century ago. Until, after decades of a life together in which neither the wife nor the husband seemed to lack anything essential, the husband, to his own surprise, almost fear, fell so intensely and forever lastingly in love that he led a double life until his last breath. Two different lives.

Now the daughter is on her way to visit the other woman in a small town on the Danube, the never-before-seen river whose course she had traced with her finger in an atlas. The suspense that has been building with the passage of time and the shrinking of the distance between what she imagined — the pictures in her mind — and the verifiable reality. But before then, the changing of trains, the waiting on a deserted platform, young people eating out of fast food containers, spilling ketchup, the local train approaching, packed with school children, and in their midst, a gray-haired, bearded teacher with a natural leather bag, who looked like a sixty-eighter, and a mutual recognition, a short conversation before changing trains again, and this time, a short stroll through the train station, later boarding the other train, and after a very short time, arriving at her destination.

This time she again spots the old lady before she sees her (because she has an eye condition common in older people), and this time she is once again wearing one of her round hats, a ladylike accessory of her generation, not dark blue like two years ago but brown, just as unflattering, though she usually never cares much about social conventions, life having taught her early on that conventions cannot halt the course of history, that they cannot be relied on, that there is nothing but emptiness behind their exemplary order. She learned very quickly, or was forced to learn at an accelerated rate, so to speak, that the only thing she could rely on was herself, her inner voice, her own abilities, that following conventions — like wearing a hat — at most served the purpose of keeping other people at bay, of making them believe that you were abiding by the rules passed down to you, adopted unseen, thus allowing you to act all the more freely, all the more independently, and, most importantly, to think. She has turned around now, and in her face you can still perceive a reflection of an emerging concern, an anxious foreboding that the person she was expecting could have missed the train or boarded the wrong one, this involuntary anticipation of something bad happening she has had for decades, ever since the war and its consequences, something bad that had never hesitated to happen and to a far greater extent than anticipated, and then that relieving smile, the young face, the hug. Finally.

Here she was at home. Here she could show the other, younger woman what she didn't know, what she couldn't have imagined. Not first and foremost this town, this small town that was rebuilt rapidly after the war, the cobblestone walkways, the small bridge over the river that flows into the Danube further down, the small square surrounded by water known as "Little Venice," the streets lined with impersonal houses, the Chinese restaurant, and on the other side of the river, the old town, small yards, old mighty trees that had survived the war, a charming riverbank, and the former convent, its baroque church, and not far away, the castle, the rocky hill, the duchess's tomb. Not first and foremost the town, the scenery, although the younger woman from far away wanted to see everything and form her own impression of everything. Plus, a mild June light bathed the small town in pastel hues, showing it at its best, and yet this light, these old trees that had survived the war without a scratch, the centuries-old course of the river would have never justified a seven-hour train ride, that required more, and besides they didn't go sightseeing until the next day, and the old lady had to let herself be talked into it. First of all, right after the younger woman arrived, right after the relief of finally seeing her, right after greeting each other, she had rushed to get home. She had waved down a taxi, which after a few minutes had stopped again, and now she was in a hurry to reach her door, running up the stairs, bounding ahead, pushing the apartment door open, "here." And "he was never here, never." And she continues, "At first, my mother was still alive. She wouldn't have understood, and then — then it was too late." She doesn't finish the thought; namely, that he had grown too old, incapable of leaving home, of traveling alone, of going away, of boarding trains, of waiting on platforms, but mainly of making a decision, of doing something on his own, of taking action, too late for any of this. Not just the older lady but especially the younger woman wished that things would have been different, that he would have been the one and not her here looking around in this barely organized collection of treasures, both great and small, that accumulate in one's lifetime: a watercolor painted by the younger woman's father, a silver-framed photo of the older woman's grandparents, one of her parents, charming glasses, small bowls, antiquarian books, photo clippings from newspapers, but mainly the overflowing bookshelves and the homemade artworks ingeniously crafted from numerous scraps of paper, colorful collages that covered the walls — except for one wall with a portrait of his face, life-sized, smiling, tender, watching over her sleep, over the last hour before falling asleep and the first hour of the morning. She, the younger woman, the visitor, she is looking at him whom she knows so well and yet seeing as if for the first time, a different man who is exactly like him in every way and yet she had never seen this expression or, much earlier in a distant past, when she sat on his lap, when she was the small fat child with the funny laugh, the "small Chinese girl" — it's a long time ago. While the man here is no longer young — his thick hair is gray white, and his hands are covered with liver spots — there is still a soft tenderness in his eyes from bygone days. Roused back to life by her, the woman. And once again, he, the small photo with the pretty frame, and next to it, another, the stern, narrow, handsome face, the deep seriousness, the large slightly protruding ears, and behind the round glasses, eyes that seem to know what will happen if he, the young man, fails to conform with the slogans, with the times, who will try not to blush for shame at the sight of himself, who calmly and without self-pity, without hate as well, seems to recognize the inevitable in a not-so-distant future, namely his own death on the front where he will be sent after he refuses to join the party, and she, holding his arm, in a light-colored dress, with her beautiful curly hair, her young face, she will support him, stick by him, and weep over him. And she too won't have to blush when she looks in the mirror. Mirror? There aren't many here. Probably she now thinks of herself as old and no longer wants to see her reflection in the mirror, see herself changed, suddenly so much older, during the long weeks she spent next to his bed, keeping a journal during the night, going back through the day hour by hour, writing down his words, his gestures, his first words in the morning, his last at night, and ultimately his final sentence. The younger woman won't read the journal, will not intrude on the couple's intimacy, not yet, not for a long time. She will merely hear the last, the final sentence, free of any confusion, of any misunderstanding, of anything superfluous, seven words spoken with complete clarity, and nothing more. One whose mastery of the language was rivaled by few availed himself of it for his last sentence, after which nothing could follow except silence. A few hours later he is dead.

"Oh dear, I'm talking too much. Would you like to see some more?" And she rummages around in an envelope, a different one than before, and she finds another photo and another, "Do you know this one?" And between the photos, a newspaper clipping, "Have you seen this picture of him?", "And this one here?", "Oh, and there, see, we were in S. in 1966," and he is wearing a somewhat flamboyant vest as if he wanted to look younger back then, or more likely, he suddenly felt younger, or maybe it was she who called out in front of a shop window, "Look, this would look good on you," and without a thought he was willing to cheat on his decidedly traditional way of dressing, adding a piece of clothing to his wardrobe which raised some eyebrows among his social circle, and which prompted his wife to remark how daring he had suddenly become. "Yes, and here, see, isn't that a pretty picture?" There are no bad photos of him. He is photogenic — his distinctive head, a Dunhill pipe often jutting from his handsome mouth, taken in her mother's venerable house in London.

And then the books he had given her. "My L.", "My dearest L." This sounds familiar to the younger woman, takes her back to her childhood, her youth, when in every book she opened at home, she found the dedication, "My B.", "My dearest B.", here now with a different letter, but signed with an unfamiliar name, a nickname, a term of affection, known only to those two, and thus a sign of intimacy, a conspiratorial closeness, secretive, even a secret itself, to be shared with no one, only much later, and then only after he was dead. There, the magnitude of the secret becomes apparent, is revealed in its entire depth and uniqueness for the astonished visitor who can only think of one thing, always the same, and who keeps repeating it to herself over and over again: how beautiful, how unique, and how difficult.

A third country in which neither the woman nor the man lived, a country that they both loved, their chosen land if a life together as a couple should ever become possible, and that country was the setting of their dream, the dream of a future together, side by side, in a remote area, in a house they could imagine down to the last detail. And the younger woman, who mainly listens, wished that the dream would have come true, but instead they waited in vain on the happy accident, on kind fate. The man remained tied down and became more and more dependent, less and less available, until in his extreme weakness and frailty he entered a retirement home, which was like an act of mercy, a few weeks in a no-man's land between life and death, and the closeness it afforded — one long goodbye. And then she was left behind, the old woman; she immersed herself in her archive of manuscripts, photographs, and printed pages. Dated and arranged, little by little they filled a suitcase, the suitcase, when people will speak of it later, which grew heavier and heavier until it was full to the brim, only capable of being closed with great difficulty, and awaiting its fate — the researcher, the historian — to reveal, view, and edit its contents, or to decide that the era contained within needn't be resurrected. She hopes, says the old lady, her many months of work have not been in vain and hasn't realized that her effort has long since been rewarded by the extension of their life together, an extension of life in the form of memories, pictures, and texts. The fate of the suitcase and its contents could scarcely interest the deceased but rather concerns the living and thereby justifies its existence, this heavy closed suitcase, keeper of a life's work, a vessel of what remains, a textual grave, while silence spreads out over the common grave in which he rests. There, the reeds sway, the birds circle, and death, once again, refuses to reveal its secret.

*

For many years she lived on the memories. They were inexhaustible and seemed to continue to increase. Thirty-three years. It wasn't until six years after his death that she took out one of his pictures again, looked deeply at his beloved face, and she could finally begin to read his letters. Although she knew certain parts of the letters by heart, his beautiful handwriting exuded a certain magic. An unmistakable handwriting that had evolved far past what he had learned in school. She read every day, every evening, and shortly before falling asleep. She couldn't get enough of them. The words, the sentences, their all-encompassing tenderness filled the apartment to the darkest corner, a bright sound that would never fall silent again. "… I am still full of the wonderful hours you gave me and eternally grateful for your love, tenderness, and consideration…" "We are always close to each other. I fall asleep with you and wake up with you. We belong together. I love you. You are my life." And all the places return and form the background to the sounds, the voice, and the words. England, over and over again. The grassy hills, the large wild park, the extensive castle. Sussex, in every season, the warmth of summer, the vibrant colors of fall, and then later, the weather, stormy and inhospitable. The evening's blazing fire. The conversations. The beginning closeness and intimacy.

"October 6, 1983. This is the 20th anniversary of our first meeting in the English summer, the beginning of a love that brought so much joy to the second half of our lives. And on this day I can only thank you for everything you have given and continue to give me, all the trouble you have gone to for me so you could share in my life and my work like no other. I'm allowed to say these things to you on this day, which will soon be followed by our familiar face-to-face conversations, from mouth to ear, and mouth to mouth. I hope to be able to take you in my arms right on the platform. And you know that my love for you is undying. I am and remain your Q." The enigmatic letter, the first letter of an English word, a cute nickname. The letters, an inexhaustible well. When he was no longer able to write, that is, when the long weeks before his death began, that is when they began to spend the days together. Now, says the old woman, now I'm waiting to see him again.

*

There is a picture that the daughter looks at several times a day. It leans against the spines of the books, a black-and-white photo. The couple. The married couple. They're standing next to each other, their shoulders almost touching, both looking in the same direction. He is showing her something, pointing with his index finger in the direction that their eyes are looking. A painting? A person? They are at a private viewing of an exhibition. Is he saying something? His mouth is slightly open. His wrinkled neck disappears into the starched collar of his striped shirt. Light falls on his mustache. There is something ambiguous in his eyes, something slightly ironic as if he has a role to play that he now, after such a long time, can no longer take entirely seriously.

The look in his wife's eyes is altogether different. They seem smaller now as if hiding in their sockets. The left eyelid is closing, but the expression is still clear. It is heartbreaking. So much hurt, such great uncertainty, complete helplessness. The daughter remembers her former pride, the way she used to beam. As if it had never existed. The mouth is also slightly open, attempting to smile. It doesn't succeed. They are standing next to each other, belong together, and yet seem to be separated. And she remembers the aged soul of this still hopeful child who will never stop believing in a miracle, in a life made of gold, far better to envision an imaginary life, *vies imaginaires.* And she hears the soft monotonous voice that calls her on the phone early in the morning to tell her how her head hurts. It's the warm föhn winds, the weather, and when she finally goes to see a doctor about these pains and her occasional bouts of dizziness, after a long talk in his practice in the country, he writes her a prescription for a medicine that she orders from a pharmacy in the nearby city, and at home, in the parlor of an old beautiful house, she drinks her tea, eats cookies, remains sitting for a moment, takes the pills from the oblong box, and begins to read, and when she gets to the words, "also for depressive moods…", she will stand up, stuff the pills and the instructions in the box, and, full of distaste and disgust, throw it in the garbage can in the kitchen. Not her. She doesn't need that sort of thing.

*

— Pain, nothing but pain. Not brief: stabbing, burning, and recently, a slowly fading scar. No. Decades long. Until my imminent death,

I'm almost 97 years old. A pain that sticks to me like a second skin I can't strip off. Always palpable, and yet invisible. I lied to all of them. What is worse, much worse, is that I tried to lie to myself. He spoke of six years, many years back. A lie I took to be the truth. To all appearances. Sometimes I was close to believing it, but I never managed to. Was it the dismissive look in his eyes, suddenly, without warning? Was it an abrupt silence, impenetrable, that stood in the room like a stone cube, taking up the entire space? Was it his after-lunch retreat as if he were somewhere else? Six years. If only I could have believed it. If only I could have managed it. Instead. I'm amazed by what people are able to bear. I was able to numb and kill the pain with sleeping pills, but they made waking up the next morning all the more terrible. The illusions of the night turned into grimaces. Waking up grew more difficult day by day. And he, as if nothing, as if nothing had ever happened, as if everything was as before. I'm not alone; there are legions of us, us women. Men? Too. But I don't know anything about them. It's the women who confide in each other. Does it help? Yes, sometimes. Briefly. I'm not the only one. It is and isn't a comfort. Doesn't everyone want to be unique and incomparable? He always used to tell me I was unique. That nobody could compare. A young, a very young love. We were barely adults. How we loved life. How fearless we were. I don't recognize myself anymore. An old, hunched-over woman, dull eyes, apathetic. And this craving for sweets. Six years, I told myself every day. Six years, I told the children. These "six years" should finally repress the reality and spread out to form a truth covering everything in an impenetrable substance. Shortly before his death he told me how much he had loved me. I carried this sentence within me; it warmed my insides and emitted a late light. He had already passed away before I suddenly realized that he had spoken the sentence in the past tense. —

*

— "Love me tender" was written there. I caught sight of the words in passing, and they grew to the size of my head, filling the passages of my brain — sometimes my head is in danger of exploding. The föhn winds, the föhn winds. I drop the coin I was holding in my hand to buy my grandson chocolate. Where is the shiny silver coin? I walk back six feet. "Love me tender" stares back at me from the newspaper rack. The coin spins one last time, heads or tails? Tails. Twenty. No number without a memory, not to mention words. Twenty, that is when we got engaged. It was 1925, and if the twenty rappen coin had landed heads up, this proud female head of our Helvetia, the mother of our country — I was once a model too, for painters and sculptors. Just like him. Like a fountain statue, athletic. I pick up the coin. Le Monde costs two francs forty. I'm buying it for my daughter. My mother tongue is French. I glance back at the words "love me tender." Which track is the train coming in on? I'm visiting my youngest grandson who worships his grandfather, the grandfather as if cast in bronze, glancing past the bustle of the ordinary. If he knew, if he only knew — I have known the man since I was sixteen. I have to put on a good front. I'd rather have a third helping of dessert and let the boy think that his grandmother is a glutton. Or does he know something? Has his mother, my daughter, told him the truth, thrown it in his face?

Doubtful. He collects the pipes his grandfather leaves him, the old Dunhill pipes with the thin crack in the dark wood of the pipe bowl, while in the distinctive head of his grandfather, when he smokes and turns page after page, memoirs, correspondence, his thoughts drift, meander — he sees right through me — and revolve around a figure in the distance. I've never seen her, the woman, the other woman. "Love me tender" and the number twenty. I'll have a third helping of dessert. I don't want to let on, don't want to destroy the boy's, my grandson's, image of his grandfather. I have the power to do it, that I still have. No, I won't, another scoop, please, and then a nap, close my eyes on the couch, rest my head on the velvet cushions that my daughter slips under me, my heavy, once proud head that hurts, the föhn winds, the föhn winds in this part of the world.

Christine Trüb, born in Berlin, grew up in Paris, Bern, Zurich and London. She studied voice, elocution, and speech therapy. Among other things, she worked as a freelance writer for the weekend supplement of the *Neue Zürcher Zeitung* and was responsible for translations and editorial work for the human rights organization Terre des hommes.

Christine Trüb lives in Zürich.

Publications

1996. *Die Häuser abgebrochen, die Gärten zugeschüttet*, short stories

1999. *Das schwimmende Wort*, short stories

2002. *Mit* Venedig beginnen, short story

2009. Ach der, novel

2011. *Die Liebe der beiden Frauen zu den Gärten*, novel

2014. *Sonntagmorgen*, short stories